Wubbzy Goes Boo!

By Maggie Testa
Based on the TV series *Wow! Wow! Wubbzy!*™ as seen on Nick Jr.™

SIMON SCRIBBLES
An imprint of Simon & Schuster Children's Publishing Division
New York   London   Toronto   Sydney
1230 Avenue of the Americas, New York, NY 10020
© 2010 Bolder Media, Inc. / Starz Media, LLC. All Rights Reserved. Wow! Wow! Wubbzy! and all related titles,
logos, and characters are trademarks of Bolder Media, Inc. / Starz Media, LLC.
All rights reserved, including the right of reproduction in whole or in part in any form.
SIMON SCRIBBLES and associated colophon are trademarks of Simon & Schuster, Inc.
For information about special discounts for bulk purchases, please contact
Simon & Schuster Special Sales at 1-866-506-1949 or business@simonandschuster.com.
Manufactured in the United States of America
0710 LAK
First Edition
2 4 6 8 10 9 7 5 3 1
ISBN 978-1-4169-9715-3

Wow! Wow! Wow! It's Halloween!
Wubbzy, Walden, and Widget love to dress up.

Crazy Costume

What do you like to dress up as for Halloween?

Draw a picture of yourself in your favorite Halloween costume.

 Walden dresses up as a Viking for the Wuzzleburg harvest festival.

Pumpkin Time!

Walden wants to know how many pumpkins are
hidden in this pile of fall leaves?

Can you count how many pumpkins there are in the leaves?

Write the number on the line below.

_____

Widget dresses up as an astronaut.

6

Blast Off!

Widget's off for a ride in her spaceship.

Connect the dots to see what her spaceship looks like.

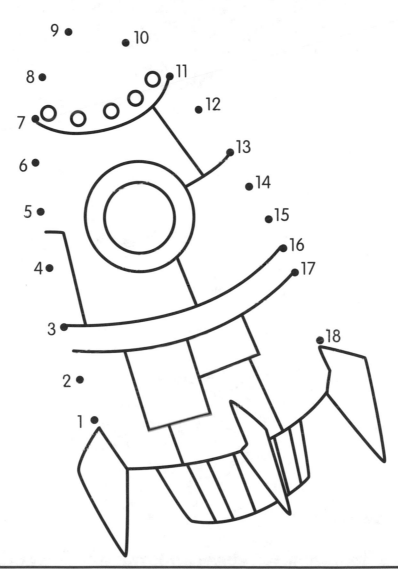

Daizy dresses up as a beautiful, flowery flower princess.

Different Daizy

Can you find five differences between the picture of Daizy below and the picture of Daizy on page 8?
Circle each one!

Wubbzy can't wait to scare everyone at the harvest festival with his costume. He's the Hairy, Scary Monster from Planet Doom!

 10

Make a Monster

If you were going to make a spooky costume for Wubbzy to wear, what would it look like?

Draw a spooky costume on the picture of Wubbzy below.

The pumpkin Ferris wheel is so much fun!

12

Festival Food
There's so much yummy food at the harvest festival.
Connect the dots to see Wubbzy's favorite treat!

 14 **Wubbzy wants to find the biggest pumpkin for the pumpkin contest.**

Big Pumpkin
Which pumpkin is the biggest?
Circle it!

Daizy names her pumpkin Pinkie Pumpkin.
She puts a pink polka-dot bow on its stem. It's so cute!

16

Pumpkin Painting

How do you like to decorate and paint your pumpkins for Halloween?

Decorate the pumpkin below any way you'd like!

Time for face painting!
"Thanks, little buddy," says Widget.

18

Paint Wubbzy's Face

Wubbzy would love it if you could decorate his face for him.

Wow! Wow! Wow! Great job!

After the harvest festival everyone changes their costume and goes dancing at the Wubb Club!

20

Loony Balloons
Do you see 10 balloons in this scene?

Circle each one you find.

Wubbzy can't wait for Halloween to come around again.
What will he dress up as next year?

Have a wubb-tastic Halloween!

23

ANSWERS

Page 5

Pumpkin Time!
Waldon wants to know how many pumpkins are
hidden in this pile of fall leaves!
Can you count how many pumpkins there are in the leaves?
Write the number on the line below.
5

Page 7

Blast Off!
Widget's off for a ride in her spaceship.
Connect the dots to see what her spaceship looks like.

Page 9

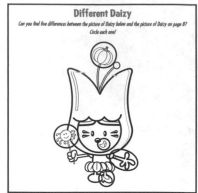

Different Daizy
Can you find five differences between the picture of Daizy below and the picture of Daizy on page 8?
Circle each one!

Page 13

Festival Food
There's so much yummy food at the harvest festival.
Connect the dots to see what Widday's favorite treat!

Page 15

Big Pumpkin
Which pumpkin is the biggest?
Circle it!

Page 21-22

Loony Balloons
Do you see 10 balloons in this scene?
Circle each one you find.

After the harvest festival everyone changes their
costume and goes dancing at the Wubb Club!

24